A Horse, Of Course!

A SUMATRA STORY

By Sibley Miller

Illustrated by Tara Larsen Chang and Jo Gershman

Feiwel and Friends

For all the BC babies—Sibley Miller

To Justin and Kailin—for unending patience and
remarkable self-reliance. I love you.
—Tara Larsen Chang

To Andy, Gabriel, and Riley. May you each find
a path in life that makes your heart sing.
—Jo Gershman

A FEIWEL AND FRIENDS BOOK
An Imprint of Macmillan

WIND DANCERS: A HORSE, OF COURSE! Copyright © 2009
by Reeves International, Inc. All rights reserved. BREYER,
WIND DANCERS, and BREYER logos are trademarks and/or registered
trademarks of Reeves International, Inc.
For information, address Feiwel and Friends,
175 Fifth Avenue, New York, N.Y. 10010.

Library of Congress Cataloging-in-Publication Data

Miller, Sibley.
A horse, of course! : a Sumatra story / by Sibley Miller ; illustrated by
Tara Larsen Chang and Jo Gershman.
p. cm. — (Wind Dancers ; #7)
Summary: After listening to adults discuss their jobs at a school career
day, the four tiny winged horses decide that they too must find work.
ISBN: 978-0-312-56402-5 (alk. paper)
[1. Magic—Fiction. 2. Horses—Fiction. 3. Occupations—Fiction.]
I. Chang, Tara Larsen, ill. II. Gershman, Jo, ill. III. Title.
PZ7.M63373Hop 2009 [Fic]—dc22 2009016141

Series editor, Susan Bishansky
Designed by Barbara Grzeslo
Feiwel and Friends logo designed by Filomena Tuosto

First Edition: 2009

P1- color

www.feiwelandfriends.com

CONTENTS

Meet the Wind Dancers · 5

CHAPTER 1 Horsework · 7

CHAPTER 2 A Walk in the Park · 17

CHAPTER 3 In the Center Ring . . . Brisa! · 28

CHAPTER 4 Sirocco the Swift · 43

CHAPTER 5 Not Quite Home on the Range · 56

CHAPTER 6 All Work and No Play? · 67

Dream Catchers · 75

CAREER DAY

At the Park

At the Circus

At the Races

On the Ranch

Meet the Wind Dancers

One day, a lonely little girl named Leanna blows on a doozy of a dandelion. To her delight and surprise, four tiny horses spring from the puff of the dandelion seeds!

Four tiny horses with shiny manes and shimmery wings. Four magical horses who can fly!

Dancing on the wind, surrounded by magic halos, they are the Wind Dancers.

The leader of the quartet is **Kona**. She has a violet-black coat and a vivid purple mane, and she flies inside a halo of magical flowers.

Brisa is as pretty as a tropical sunset with her coral-pink color and blonde mane and tail. Magical jewels make up Brisa's halo, and she likes to admire her gems (and herself) every time she looks in a mirror.

Sumatra is silvery blue with sea-green wings. Much like the ocean, she can shift from calm to stormy in a hurry! Her magical halo is made up of ribbons, which flutter and dance as she flies.

The fourth Wind Dancer is—surprise!—a colt. His name is Sirocco. He's a fiery gold, and he likes to go-go-go. Everywhere he goes, his magical halo of butterflies goes, too.

The tiny flying horses live together in the dandelion meadow in a lovely house carved out of the trunk of an apple tree. Every day, Leanna wishes she'll see the magical little horses again. (She's sure they're nearby, but she doesn't know they're invisible to people.) And the Wind Dancers get ready for their next adventure.

CHAPTER 1

Horsework

"What should we do today?" Sumatra asked her fellow Wind Dancers, as they took flight over the dandelion meadow one bright sunny morning.

But before anyone could answer, Sumatra had an idea of her own. "How about a dance-off?" she suggested. "We could dance 'til we drop. Last one flying gets a pumpkin cake!"

"Well, we all know who would win *that* contest, don't we?" Kona responded. "You!"

"Okay," Sumatra said, rubbing her front hooves together eagerly and looking around.

"How about . . . hey!"

"Hay?" Brisa asked primly. "What's fun about hay?"

"I think hay's yummy!" Sirocco declared. "Especially if it's dripping in honey!"

Sumatra shook her head.

"Not *hay*!" she scoffed. "*Hey*! As in, hey, what's going on down there at Leanna's school?"

The other Wind Dancers turned to look. As they'd been flying, they'd come to the big red-brick building that was their friend Leanna's school. But today, there were a lot more grown-ups there than usual at the start of the day.

"What are all those adults doing here?" Sumatra asked curiously. "Don't they have jobs to go to?"

"*Jobs?*" Brisa said. "You mean like how it's Kona's job to make us our apple muffins every morning, and Sirocco's job to sweep the kitchen floor with his tail after breakfast, and *my* job to look really pretty?"

"Not quite," Sumatra said dryly. "People have jobs that take much longer than a floor-sweeping. Lots of them go to an office all day."

"Being beautiful is an all-day job, too," Brisa noted.

"Uh-huh," Kona said, just as dryly as Sumatra had. Then she turned to Sumatra with interest in her coal-black eyes. "What do the grown-ups *do* in these offices?"

"You know, they *work* and stuff," Sumatra said vaguely.

"What *kind* of stuff?" Sirocco asked. As the children and grown-ups began to file into the school, he landed on the windowsill of Leanna's classroom, followed by Sumatra, Kona, and Brisa.

Before Sumatra could come up with an answer for Sirocco, Leanna's teacher spoke up.

"Class," she announced, "as you already know, today is Career Day! Several of your parents have come in to tell us about their different lines of work."

Sumatra nickered. *Work*! There was that mysterious word again.

"We'll start with Cassie's mom, Dr. Withers," the teacher said, motioning at a dark-haired lady in a long, white coat. "She's a large-animal veterinarian."

"That's right!" Dr. Withers said, smiling as she moved to the front of the classroom. "Some of you have seen me at your farms, helping out your cows, pigs, and horses when they get sick."

The Wind Dancers exchanged excited looks.

"She helps horses!" Brisa exclaimed. "She's an *us* doctor!"

"Neat!" Sumatra said.

Clearly, Leanna and her classmates thought so, too. Everyone began asking Dr. Withers questions like, "How do you take a horse's temperature?" and "What's your favorite animal?" and "Is your office in a barn?!"

The Wind Dancers settled in on their windowsill, eagerly listening to everything Dr. Withers had to say. By the time the next grown-up—a tack and feed store owner— spoke, the little horses were hooked!

. . .

When the morning ended—and Leanna's class trooped to the cafeteria for lunch—the Wind Dancers launched themselves off the window-sill. Their faces were thoughtful, and the flowers, ribbons, jewels, and butterflies in their magic halos were bright and bouncy.

"Mystery solved!" Sumatra said with satisfaction. "Now we know what grown-ups do when they go off to work."

"They fly planes!" Sirocco said, doing an excited flip in the air.

"They take lovely pictures for shiny magazines!" Brisa said dreamily.

"They boss people around in tall office towers!" Kona said with awe in her voice.

Sumatra frowned. Now that this whole "work" concept was cleared up, another idea was troubling her.

"Okay," she posed to her friends. "That's what *they* do. But what do *we* do?"

"Go for lunch, I hope," Sirocco crowed. "I'm hungry!"

"Oh, Sirocco," Brisa giggled. "You're *always* hungry."

"No, seriously," Sumatra said. "What are *our* jobs? We can't just *play* every day!"

"Even children have jobs, when you think about it," Kona agreed with a sage nod. "They go to school and learn things!"

"Maybe you don't have to have a job if you're *magic*," Sirocco said, popping one of his enchanted butterflies out of his halo and watching with satisfaction as a new one fizzed back in.

"And as I already said," Brisa reminded her friends, "*my* job is to fill the world with beauty."

"Just *being* magic or beautiful doesn't seem like a job," Kona said, biting her lip.

"I know," Sumatra agreed with a frown. Then suddenly, an idea occurred to her.

"Let's have our own Career Day!" she declared. "We could each decide what we want *our* jobs to be!"

"Oh, that's easy," Sirocco said. "I want to be an astronaut and fly to the moon!"

"Ooh," Brisa laughed. "And *I* want to be a clothing designer and make beautiful gowns!"

"I'll be a teacher," Kona said

with a determined nod. "I think folks could learn a *lot* from me!"

"I don't know about *that*," Sirocco said, "but you're *definitely* bossy enough to lead a classroom!"

"No," Sumatra protested. "Kona can't be a teacher."

"Hey!" Kona pouted. "I am *too* smart enough to be a teacher!"

"I'm not saying you're not smart," Sumatra said, giving Kona a quick nose  nuzzle. "It's just that you're a horse! An *invisible-to-people* horse. Even if school-kids could see you, they wouldn't understand your neighs and whinnies. And Sirocco, I think you'd be too little to fit into a space suit. They're made for grown-ups."

"Oh, yeah," Sirocco said sadly. "I guess I

didn't think of that."

"And Brisa," Sumatra said, turning to the coral-pink filly, "I'm afraid sewing machines and *hooves* don't mix."

Brisa shrugged cheerfully.

"I guess I'll just have to go back to Plan A," she chirped. "Professional beauty!"

"No, wait!" Sumatra said. "There *are* jobs we could do. Horsy jobs! Think about our friends the big horses—they get saddled up all the time so their owners can ride them."

"So we just need to find careers that are good for horses!" Kona added.

"Sounds like fun!" Sirocco said, clicking his hooves together eagerly.

Sumatra's green eyes gleamed.

"It sounds," she declared, "like our day's adventure!"

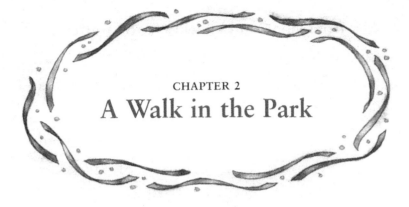

CHAPTER 2
A Walk in the Park

No sooner had Sumatra decided on the Wind Dancers' mission than Kona spotted something intriguing, if not exactly *career-ish*.

The violet-black filly watched people tromping along every sidewalk and path. She saw little children skipping alongside their parents, and school-kids on lunchtime field trips. Most of them carried blankets or lawn chairs, not to mention picnic baskets or lunch bags.

And they were *all* walking in the same direction—to the park!

Kona gave her friends a little wave with

her front hoof and quickly drifted after the crowd. She *had* to see what they were up to!

Kona loved the park. It was just like nature, but . . . not.

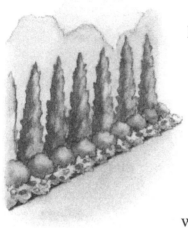

While there were plenty of tall trees, colorful flowers, and shapely shrubs, they were all lined up in nice, even rows and neatly trimmed, instead of running wild the way they did in the dandelion meadow.

What's more, the ponds were square and not muddy.

And the pathways were smooth and paved.

In other words, the park was a very orderly place. And Kona *loved* orderly places.

As Kona flew deeper into the park, she

saw that it was packed with people!

"Something's happening!" Kona breathed.

Before long, she knew *just* what that something was. Kona heard it before she saw it—the *twang* of a guitar, the *zing* of a violin, and the *badum, bum, bum* of a drum.

"It's a concert!" Kona declared happily. "Maybe I'll listen for just a few minutes before I go searching for my horse career."

She zipped ahead and ducked beneath some low-hanging trees. She emerged on the big, open lawn in the center of the park. Around a little, circular stage, people were enjoying the band's jazzy music.

Kona was, too! She almost forgot about her career-finding adventure, until she spotted something *else* that made her gasp.

It was a horse! A solid-looking, chestnut brown quarter horse, looking regal as he stood on the edge of the crowd.

Standing next to the big gelding was an officer in crisp navy blue with knee-high boots, a helmet, and a shiny, gold badge over her breast pocket.

Before she could think twice about it, Kona zipped right up to the gelding and fluttered excitedly before his eyes. She expected the big horse to gasp in surprise, the way most animals did when they first saw a tiny, flying horse. (After all, it wasn't every day that one came face-to-face with magic!)

But the gelding merely snorted and said, "Move aside, miss! I'm working here. Keeping the peace. *Hup, hup!*"

Startled, Kona immediately obeyed and fluttered out of the horse's view.

But she didn't fly away. She couldn't! Not after hearing what the big quarter horse had said: *"I'm working here!"*

"You have a *job*?" Kona breathed in the big horse's ear.

"Of course I have a job!" the gelding rasped in his deep voice. "I'm a police horse! Law and order! *That's* my job!"

"But . . ." Kona replied with a frown, "what exactly does that mean?"

Again the horse snorted.

"Follow me, recruit," he declared.

Then he made a loud rumble and began

trotting toward a pretty bed of flowers. A few boys were laughing and wrestling among the colorful blooms, knocking many of them off their stems, and flattening others.

"Oh, those poor flowers!" Kona fretted. The magic flowers in her halo cringed, too.

"You there!" the police horse neighed at the boys. "Move it along now! *Hup, hup*!"

The boys froze in mid-grapple and gazed up at the very large horse looming over them. Then they squealed, scrambled to their feet, and ran back to the grass where they were supposed to be.

"Wow!" Kona breathed.

"See what I mean?" the gelding responded. "Nobody argues with a Very Big Horse!"

"Nobody?" Kona asked incredulously.

"If they do, they get a ticket!" the gelding replied with an extra-loud snort.

Kona was stunned! Whatever the big horse told people to do—they did!

"Being a police horse is like bossy-hooves heaven!" Kona said to the gelding. Then she cleared her throat. "Not that I'm bossy or anything!"

"What's wrong with being bossy?" the gelding demanded.

Kona felt her heart sing! Clearly, police horse was the perfect career for her! Grinning, Kona began scanning the park, along with the gelding.

"Do you see any pets pilfering picnic food?" she asked the police horse. "Mockingbirds mocking someone? Cats catfighting?"

"I've got my hooves full with all these pesky people," the police horse replied, as he began trotting toward a litterbug. "But more power to you, recruit. Go forth and keep the peace. Law and order! *Hup, hup!*"

Before Kona knew it, her friend was gone.

Which meant keeping the peace in the animal world was *all* up to her!

Kona puffed out her chest with pride. Then she began zipping around the park, looking for critter crime.

It didn't take her long to find it! In the same flower bed where the gelding had caught the wrestlers, Kona spotted a fountain of black soil spraying into the air.

"*Hmmm!*" Kona said, as she zipped down to the garden to investigate.

Sure enough, an animal was at fault. Specifically, a chipmunk! He was scrabbling at the dirt with his paws, sending dirt and flowers up behind him.

"*What* are you doing?" Kona whinnied, landing in the dirt next to the little rodent. The chipmunk stopped digging for a moment to glance at her. He was holding a giant nut in his mouth.

"Um, what I meant to say," Kona said, trying to look stern, "was *hup, hup*! You there. You're damaging park property!"

Instead of retreating in shame, though, the chipmunk shrugged and kept on digging.

"Hey!" Kona cried. "You can't do that!"

But by the time she'd finished protesting, the chipmunk had dropped his nut into his fresh dirt hole and covered the treasure up.

"But, but," Kona stuttered, "I *told* you not to dig up the flower bed!"

With his mouth nut-free, the chipmunk could finally respond.

"Well, I'm telling *you*, horsy," the animal chittered, "that I'm a chipmunk. We find nuts, see? We dig holes and bury 'em. When winter comes, I'm gonna dig this nut *back* up and eat it for dinner. And there's nothing you and your sparkly little wings can do about it!"

Kona was so shocked, she could barely speak. Which didn't matter anyway because the law-breaking chipmunk had scampered away, chittering cheekily as he went.

"Well . . . well . . ." Kona sputtered, "I'll just have to find another creature to curtail."

The rest of Kona's day went pretty much the way of the chipmunk. When she ticketed a robin for trying to build its nest in the park's stage area, instead of in a tree, the robin thanked her for the nice birch bark that she could use for her nest.

And when she tried to get some honeybees to stop buzzing so loudly, one of them stung her!

"I don't get it!" Kona declared as she licked at the throbbing welt on her foreleg. "Everybody listens to the big police horse!"

"Every *human*," another (loudly) buzzing bee corrected her. "But animals? We abide by the laws of nature—not bossy-hoof horses!"

"I am *not* bossy—" Kona began, before she cut herself off with a sigh.

"Oh, what's the use?" she asked herself. "Clearly, the only place I can keep order in is our apple tree house. My career of busting baddies is a total bust!"

CHAPTER 3
In the Center Ring . . . Brisa!

When Kona had dashed to the park, Brisa had darted away as well.

She'd spotted some pretty colors winking and blinking at her from the far edge of town.

And when Brisa spotted something pretty, she was powerless to resist (even if she was supposed to be looking for a career that was about *more* than beauty).

"*Tra, la, la, la,*" Brisa warbled as she flew toward the spots of color.

As she got closer, she saw that the colors— lemon yellow, tangerine, and sky blue—were triangular flags!

When she was even closer, Brisa realized that the flags were attached to the poles of a giant, striped tent! Excited children with adults streamed through the opening.

"Oh!" Brisa cried. "What *is* this place?"

She zipped over the peoples' heads into the tent. Once inside, she gasped in awe.

Brisa saw three bright-striped rings laid out in the sawdust-covered floor, glittery trapezes hung near towering platforms, and cartoony clowns warming up the crowd.

It was a circus!

An instant later, Brisa couldn't see *anything*, because a beam of light had just flashed in her eyes!

The coral-pink filly darted to the side and blinked away the spots dancing before her eyes.

She looked around the tent in confusion, until she saw a small canvas doorway toward the back. The tent flap was propped open and sparkly light was spilling through it.

"Ooh!" Brisa exclaimed with curiosity. She zipped through the tent flap, and gasped.

She was backstage!

There were performers stretching their muscles and warming up their voices.

There were monkeys and baby elephants having pre-circus snacks.

And everywhere Brisa looked, there were *mirrors* surrounded by giant lightbulbs. Plus costumes decorated with rhinestones and sequins.

Every time the light hit the sequins and stones, beams of color bounced into the air.

"This is what made me see stars out in

the big top," Brisa said. "I was blinded by beauty! Speaking of which, it's been at least an hour since I looked in a mirror."

Brisa saw a particularly large make-up mirror in one corner and flew over to it, intending to give her mane a quick comb.

But the moment she fluttered in front of the glass, a musical voice jangled her.

"Ex-*cuse* me," the voice said. "But that mirror is reserved for the *star* of the circus. And the star of the circus is me! I'll thank you to keep your sparkly little self out of my way!"

Brisa gasped, flitted away from the mirror, and looked down at the speaker.

The *horsy* speaker.

"*Ooooh!*" Brisa cried.

She was gazing down at a filly who was more beautiful than any spangled costume.

The graceful Percheron had a snowy-white coat and silvery gray mane and tail, which was woven with pink ribbon.

Between her ears, the big horse wore a red feather. And her hooves were painted pink!

Aware of Brisa's stunned admiration, the filly preened.

"Go on and say it," she said indulgently.

"Say what?" Brisa asked with wide eyes.

"What *everybody* says when they first

meet me," the filly said. "'You're TrixieBelle
LaRue, the world-famous circus horse!'"

"TrixieBelle?" Brisa breathed. It was the
most beautiful name she'd ever heard.
"Circus horse?"

"Wait a minute," TrixieBelle said, as she
squinted at Brisa. "Do you mean to say you
haven't heard of me?"

Brisa shook her head no. But before the sparkly filly could feel insulted, Brisa rushed to add, "But I don't have to know you to know that you have the *perfect* career for me! I want to be a circus horse just like you!"

TrixieBelle paused and gave Brisa a hard look. Brisa shook her blonde mane as TrixieBelle took in the little Wind Dancer's jeweled necklace and magical halo, along with her shimmery coral-pink coat.

"You *do* have a certain something," TrixieBelle admitted. "You remind me of myself when I was a foal."

"Plus, I have wings!" Brisa pointed out helpfully.

"Yes," TrixieBelle said casually. "Some of us need wings to dance on air, I suppose. Me? Not so much!"

"Still, do you think I have what it takes to be a circus horse?" Brisa asked breathlessly.

"We'll see, sweetie," TrixieBelle said absently. She turned to gaze into the mirror. "Now leave me be, please. I must prepare for my performance."

Brisa grinned!

So must I! she thought to herself.

. . .

A little while later—after a dip into a rack of spangled costumes and circus-performer make-up—Brisa was big-top ready!

Around her neck, she wore a fan-like collar of fuzzy feathers. Her hooves glimmered with her multi-colored magical jewels. And she'd woven her mane and tail into glittery braids. She was a show horse like none other!

Well, like *one* other.

Fluttering over to TrixieBelle, who was standing at the entrance to the main tent, Brisa announced, "Miss LaRue! I'm ready for my close-up!"

TrixieBelle whinnied in surprise, staring at a Brisa who was so weighted down, she had trouble staying in the air.

"*What* have you done to yourself?" the circus horse demanded of Brisa.

But before Brisa could answer, she was interrupted by the ringmaster's voice, which was booming through the big top!

"And now, ladies and gentleman," the

ringmaster announced, "please direct your gaze to the center ring, where you will behold the very picture of equine excellence, acrobat and dancer on air *TrixieBelle LaRue!*"

"We'll talk later," TrixieBelle said to Brisa.

"Sure!" Brisa chirped. "Right after our performance!"

"*Our* performance?" TrixieBelle gasped.

But there was no time to argue. It was time for the show!

TrixieBelle pranced into the center ring, tossing her mane proudly.

Brisa darted behind her, wobbling a bit in the air as she hauled her heavy collar and gem-weighted hooves along with her.

"Oh, I wish I wasn't invisible to people," Brisa sighed. "Then the audience could see my beautiful costume."

"Shhh," TrixieBelle admonished her. "I have to focus on my act!"

To the sound of a drum roll, TrixieBelle launched herself onto her hind legs and began scooting around the circus ring, waving her forelegs in the air.

She was amazing!

When TrixieBelle had dropped back to all fours, she sank into a deep curtsey.

The audience roared and Brisa clopped her hooves together right along with them.

"That was very nice!" Brisa complimented the big filly. "Now it's *my* turn!"

Brisa reared back in the air, fluttering her front hooves daintily.

At least, she *tried* to be dainty. But her costume was so unwieldy that she tumbled into an awkward backflip!

"Whoops!" Brisa giggled when she had regained her balance. "That didn't go *quite* the way I planned it, but at least my collar is still fluffy!"

She blew a few feathers out of her face,
then she sank into a shaky imitation of
TrixieBelle's curtsey.

"Ta da!" she announced.

"*Ta da?*" TrixieBelle sputtered out of the
side of her mouth. "Talk about putting the cart
before the horse!"

"What do you mean?" Brisa asked. But TrixieBelle didn't answer. She was too busy doing her next move.

She scampered up onto a giant ball and balanced on top of it! Then she rolled the ball—and her- self—in a perfect circle around the ring.

"Oooh!" Brisa exclaimed. "Now me!"

The moment TrixieBelle pranced off the ball, Brisa hopped on.

And she stayed on, for about half a second.

"Ta-*daaaa*!" she squealed as she scrabbled down the side of the ball and landed on the ground with a *splat*! The impact sent glitter and jewels flying!

"My costume!" Brisa wailed.

TrixieBelle galloped over and gasped.

"Who cares about your costume!" Trixie-

Belle neighed at the tiny horse. "What about *my* performance!? I can't risk doing my next bit—a side shuffle—with jewels in my way! I could trip and fall!"

"Oh, the audience wouldn't mind!" Brisa scoffed. "Not when you *look* so pretty."

"Being a show horse *isn't* just about pretty," TrixieBelle scolded. "It's about stunning feats of performance! It's about talent. And it's about *hard work*."

"Oh," Brisa said quietly. She hung her head. "Oh, I see."

"I suppose I'll have to cut my act short," TrixieBelle sighed, beginning to trot off-stage.

"No, don't!" Brisa cried. "There is *one* thing I can do very well and that's magic!"

She used her wings to scoop her jewels into a little pile. Then she popped each one back into her magic halo: *fizz, fizz, fizz!*

In an instant, TrixieBelle's stage was

cleared. The snowy Percheron nodded at Brisa, then launched into the rest of her act.

Meanwhile, flying toward the ring's edge, Brisa squirmed out of her huge, feathery collar.

"So being beautiful isn't enough to make me a circus horse," Brisa said to herself, a bit sadly. But then she brightened, as TrixieBelle finished her act with a flourish.

"*Someday* I'll figure out how to be a circus horse!" Brisa promised herself, as she waved to TrixieBelle and flew out of the circus tent, headed for home.

CHAPTER 4
Sirocco the Swift

Sirocco *knew* he should be looking for a career, just as the fillies were. A responsible, grown-up horsy job.

"But how can I think about work," Sirocco asked himself, "when I'm so *hungry?*"

"Here's an idea," he continued, as he zipped through the sky, "whichever I find first—a job or lunch—that's what I'll go for."

No sooner had the words left his mouth when Sirocco smelled something.

Something warm and toasty.

"Yum!" Sirocco declared. "I guess that

settles it. Lunch it is! Now if I can just find where that delish smell is coming from . . ."

Sirocco sniffed the air carefully, following his nose as he flew.

"Hmm!" Sirocco said, reaching a place that was open to the air and filled with rows of bleachers packed with people. And many of those people were eating salty—

"Pretzels!" Sirocco cried in delight. "It's my lucky day. Now I just have to figure out how to get my hooves on one and—"

Wah-wah-WAH-wahwahwah-WAH-wah!

A bugle call startled Sirocco out of his foodie fantasy. He froze!

Suddenly, he realized *why* all those people were sitting in bleachers.

The stair-step seats faced a big, dirt track.

And *onto* that track were trotting *big horses*! A whole parade of sleek, slim, muscled thoroughbreds!

Each horse stepped into a starting gate.

Then a horn blew even louder than the bugle. The horses darted out of their starting gates and began galloping around the track!

Sirocco was so dazzled, he forgot all about pretzels.

"That stallion likes speed as much as I do!" Sirocco exclaimed, following a racing horse toward the back of the pack. He spotted the number eight on the horse's saddle blanket and looked at a scoreboard.

"His name is Sebastian Steed!" Sirocco said. "Cool!"

Sirocco began to cheer along with all the other race fans.

"Come on, Sebastian Steed!" he neighed. "You can do it!"

Sirocco did loop-de-loops high above the track. He pumped his hooves and whinnied.

"Go, go, *go*, Sebastian Steed!" he cried.

To Sirocco's shock, Sebastian Steed began to go indeed! He swung to the inside of the pack of pounding horses and began to inch forward. He passed Horse Number Three. He passed Number Six. He passed Two, and Five.

And in the final stretch, Sebastian Steed passed the remaining horses! He thrust his nose out impossibly far and crossed the finish line—first!

"Hooray, Sebastian Steed!" Sirocco

neighed. In his excitement, he darted down to the track, straight to the champ.

"Awesome race, Sebastian Steed!" Sirocco whinnied. "You're even cooler than a hot pretzel!"

"I will be in just a minute," the racehorse muttered, as his trainer aimed a hose of nice, cold water at him.

"*Aaaaaah!*" he moaned as the water washed sweat and dirt from his coat. "That's better. Now *who* are you, squirt?"

Sirocco frowned.

"Well, I know I'm little," he admitted. "But check out *these*!"

He fluttered his wings at Sebastian Steed.

"They're made for speed!"

"Don't tell me you want to get into the racing game, too?" the stallion said.

"Sure, I got it in me!" Sirocco declared. "Hey, do you get to eat pretzels every day when you're a racehorse?"

"Junk food? Have *you* got the wrong idea!" Sebastian Steed said with a laugh. "Walk with me, kid. I've got to stretch these legs before I hit the winner's circle. Then I get my rubdown."

Respectfully, Sirocco flew next to the stallion's head as the big horse loped around the inner field.

"So, how did you start racing, Big S?" Sirocco asked the stallion. "What happens after you win? I bet they let you spend *lots* of time living the good life!"

"I live the good life, sure," the stallion said. "*After* I put in hours of training every day and eat a healthy diet and—"

Wah-wah-WAH-wahwahwah-WAH-wah!

Sirocco jumped. The bugle was calling. Another race was about to begin!

"Can you hold that thought?" he asked Sebastian Steed. "I've got some business to take care of."

Sirocco eyed the starting gate, as some racetrack workers rolled it back out onto the track.

"Now, squirt," Sebastian warned. "You don't want to jump into the race, do you?"

"Hello?" Sirocco said, fluttering his wings so hard they hummed. "Do you even have to ask? I've beaten *hummingbirds* in races. This career is *made* for me!"

"Maybe it is, maybe it isn't," Sebastian replied. "To find out, you've got to train!"

"Trust me, Big S," Sirocco said. "I've got all I need. Not to mention a great racehorse

name. I just came up with it! *Sirocco the Swift!* Like it?"

"Subtle," Sebastian said dryly. "But seriously. You *really* don't know what you're getting into—"

Sirocco saw the next batch of racehorses trotting up to their gates.

"Listen, Big S," he interrupted. "Can we talk later? How about in the winner's circle!"

Before Sebastian Steed could protest any more, Sirocco zipped toward the starting gates!

"Hi, there!" Sirocco introduced himself to a black filly in the first gate. She looked away.

So, Sirocco tried the colt in the next gate.

"My name's Sirocco the Swift—"

"Buzz off, butterfly," the horse muttered.

"Butterfly!?" Sirocco whispered to himself. "Of all the nerve! Oh . . ."

Sirocco cast a guilty glance at the butterflies fluttering in his magic halo.

"Sorry, guys," he said. Then he went further down the line of gates.

"That big horse will be eating his words when he sees me win this race!" Sirocco murmured to himself.

He placed himself between the heads of two other horses. Then—

HONK!

The race began! As the big horses shot out of their gates, Sirocco flew right above—and suddenly *behind*—their heads.

"*Whoa!*" the flying colt yelled. "You guys don't waste any time, do you?"

Of course, none of the thoroughbreds answered him. They just continued to thunder down the track, so that Sirocco found himself flying through a cloud of dust and dirt!

"I like a mud pie as much as the next horse," Sirocco huffed as he continued to trail the pack, "but this is ridiculous!"

"Only another lap to go, folks!" boomed the voice on the loudspeaker. "And Willie the Kid is in the lead!"

"Uh-oh!" Sirocco said indignantly. "That's supposed to be *my* name he's announcing. I better catch up!"

Sirocco grit his teeth and buzzed after the

pack. He had no doubt that he could catch up to them. And *win*!

Sure enough, Sirocco soon overtook the last horse in the pack.

"See ya!" Sirocco giggled as he whizzed by the horse. "Wouldn't want to be ya!"

Sirocco plunged into the herd. But they were so tightly packed together, he had to veer right and left to avoid being tangled up in a flying tail or batted by a flapping ear!

Sirocco's wings began burning with effort.

He was suddenly too out of breath to quip.

But a quick glance at the winner's circle— where Sebastian Steed was being draped with a blanket of flowers—made Sirocco forget his aches and pains.

Squinting fiercely, he flew faster than he ever had before! He inched forward a little. And a little more! But just when Sirocco was sure he was going to pull ahead—

"*Whaaaaaaa!*" the tiny colt neighed.

Sirocco found himself hurtling through the air—but now going in the wrong direction! He'd been tossed out of the race by a gust of wind.

He landed with a loud *oof* in the soft dirt at the edge of the track.

Sirocco then watched, heartbroken and humiliated, as the big horses pounded to the finish line without him.

"And the winner is . . ." the announcer boomed.

Sirocco dipped his head and pressed his front knees over his ears. He didn't want to hear the winner's name if it wasn't *his* name!

When he regained himself, Sirocco flapped slowly into the air. He gazed sorrowfully at the winner's circle. Now that this race was over, Sebastian Steed was being led through a trophy ceremony.

"Sebastian was right," Sirocco whispered, hanging his head. "I wasn't ready. I didn't deserve to win!"

The flying colt now knew that the only way he *could* succeed as a racehorse was to train and train *hard*. But his wings ached. His flank was bruised from his tumble. And his pride hurt most of all!

Which is why he flew straight out of the racetrack. He didn't wait to say good-bye to Sebastian Steed. He didn't even get himself a pretzel!

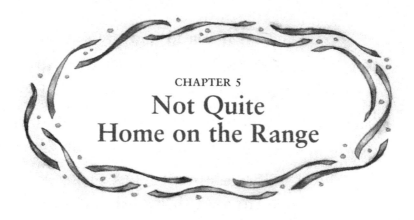

CHAPTER 5

Not Quite Home on the Range

"Empty grass hills," Sumatra muttered to herself, as she flew beyond the dandelion meadow. "How am I going to find a career in a whole lot of nothing?"

But before long, she found herself singing.

"*Oh, give me a home, where the Wind Dancers roam,*" she warbled as she gazed out at the prairie. "*Where the cows and the big horses play* . . . Hey, wait a minute!"

Sumatra suddenly realized that she wasn't just *making up* her little ditty. She was inspired by something she'd just spotted off in the distance! A crowd of mooing cows nestled between a grassy hill and a rambling ranch. The ranch consisted of a small bunkhouse, a medium-sized barn, and a big paddock surrounded by a split-log fence.

"The barn must be where those cows live when they're not grazing in the valley," Sumatra said to herself.

But even *more* interesting than all the mooing cows was the *big horse* cantering easily among them!

"Looks to me like that horse is working!"

Sumatra said triumphantly. She began racing eagerly over the hills until she reached the pinto, who was a rangy mare.

"Hello!" Sumatra nickered when the mare paused for a moment in her cow herding. "I'm Sumatra! A Wind Dancer!"

"Well, hi there, you cute little thing," the pinto said in a lilting twang. "I'm Sassafras, a cow horse. But *you*! A flying horse? I never!"

"Well, *I* never met a real, live cow horse either!" Sumatra admitted with a grin. "So, I guess that makes two of us. I'd love to hear all about your job—"

"Excuse me," the cow horse drawled. "It looks like some of our cows have broken off from the herd. I've got to go rustle 'em back. I'll be back faster than a bronco can buck!"

Sassafras neighed the last words over her shoulder as she galloped up the hill, where a few lonely cows were looking lost.

Sassafras whinnied loudly. She galloped around the confused cattle until, somehow, she nudged them back to the group.

Then Sassafras trotted casually back over to Sumatra.

"So, is this your first time out on the range?" the cow horse asked the Wind Dancer. "How do you like it?"

"So much that . . . I want to make a career out of it!" Sumatra declared without a moment's hesitation. "Your job is perfect for me! I mean, when I neigh, animals listen! I even directed a talent show recently!"

"Well, that's a great start," Sassafras said with a twinkle in her eye. "But how do you feel about living life on the prairie? Smelling the sweet grass? Listening to the cowpokes as they sing songs, cook beans, and toast marshmallows over an open fire?"

Sumatra's eyes twinkled right back.

"This is the life for me!" she replied.

"Well, it's not *all* cowgirl songs and riding the open range," Sassafras cautioned. "We run a tight herd out here. Each cow can eat more than a hundred pounds of grass per day, so I have to keep them on the move."

"That's a *lot* of grass," Sumatra said.

"Sure is!" Sassafras drawled. "That's why the cows need *me* to lead them to it. And when they wander, I rustle 'em back. They'd be lost without a cow horse to guide 'em!"

Sumatra grinned.

"Then I *definitely* want to help!"

Filled with excitement and determination, Sumatra flew high above the cows and noticed that a couple of calves had scampered away from the herd. Their mothers followed them, munching grass while they kept an eye on their little ones.

"A-*ha*!" Sumatra said triumphantly. She buzzed down to the mama cows and whinnied at them.

"All right, ladies!" she said. "It's time to rejoin the herd."

"Mooooooo," one of the cows said to her, blinking her long lashes lazily. She nipped up another tuft of grass and planted her feet firmly on the ground.

"All right," Sumatra whispered to herself.

"If reasoning won't work, I'll try rustling!"

"*Yahoo!*" Sumatra shouted. She flew circles around the mama cows, trying to edge them back toward the herd.

When Sassafras had done this, the cows had scampered out of her way. But with tiny Sumatra, the cattle just stood their ground.

"*Grrr,*" Sumatra grumbled—until she spotted the calves, who were scampering around the grass playfully.

"I know what to do," she told herself. "I should just rustle the calves! They're smaller. And if I can get them to rejoin the herd, their mamas will follow. I'm sure of it!"

Sumatra flew right up to the cute cows.

She flew over their heads and under their bellies. She whinnied and neighed. She did *everything* she could think of to move the babies back to their brood!

But the calves only bleated at her cutely.

And then, they ran *away* from the herd.

"No!" Sumatra whinnied after them.

Her head low, Sumatra flew back to Sassafras, who was chortling kindly.

"They're not listening to me!" Sumatra whinnied.

"Aw, don't be sad, sugar!" the pinto said to her tiny new friend. "It took me a while to get the hang of this job, too. I started training when I was just a filly. My cowgirl taught me all sorts of skills, from cutting the herd in half to rustling the cows into their paddock to roping a stubborn steer. It took me *years* to become the cow horse I am today!"

"So, you think there's a chance for me?" Sumatra asked hopefully.

"Sure!" Sassafras said. "Or . . ."

"Or what?" Sumatra asked warily.

"Or maybe cowpokin' just isn't the right career for you," Sassafras said simply.

"Oh, but I want to be a cow horse!" Sumatra said. "I really, really do!"

"Maybe yes, maybe no. You just got here, after all!" Sassafras said with a smile. "And you don't *have* to decide today. You're just a young one yourself. You could find a zillion other things to be before you grow up!"

"But—" Sumatra protested.

"Listen," Sassafras interrupted her. "Your job right now is to dream! And imagine! And play! You're only a filly. You've got plenty of time to think about work."

Sumatra's green-lashed eyes went wide.

"I guess I never thought of it that way," she realized.

"Now, c'mon," Sassafras went on. "Let *me* rustle up the rascally calves and their mamas and then we'll settle down to eat."

"Okay!" Sumatra said with a grin.

But when she met up with the mare at the campfire a few minutes later, Sumatra felt a pang in her belly—one that was more than just hunger. She turned to the pinto, who was lapping water out of a tin bucket.

"You know, Sassafras," she admitted, "I'd love to stay, but I have *another* job to do—at home!"

"Well, get along, then," Sassafras said with a sweet smile. "But come back and visit sometime, you hear?"

"I promise!" Sumatra said with a grateful good-bye grin at her new friend.

CHAPTER 6
All Work and No Play?

"Kona! Brisa! Sirocco!"

Sumatra whinnied to her friends with delight, as all the Wind Dancers arrived back at the apple tree house.

What a day's adventure it had been!

Kona was holding a stack of birch bark tickets in her teeth and looking a bit sheepish.

Brisa's face was

streaked with make-up and her mane was tangled with glitter and sagging feathers.

And Sirocco was covered in mud, not to mention bumps and bruises!

Hmmm, Sumatra thought to herself slyly. She tried to squelch a giggle that was welling up in the back of her throat.

"How was your day?" she asked Kona, Brisa, and Sirocco.

Kona spat out her birch bark and declared, "I decided to be a police horse!"

"Ooh, really?!" Sumatra said, trying not

to let her eyes twinkle. "Tell me about it!"

"Well, you know . . ." Kona said, glancing with shifty eyes at her friends. "Policing is all about keeping law and order. Making sure no animals steal or disturb the peace. I even gave out birch bark tickets to bad guys!"

"So basically, you're the same bossy-hooves at work that you are at home?" Sirocco said with a gleam in his eyes.

Before Kona could retort, Brisa asked her a question.

"Kona, if you gave *away* tickets," she wondered, "why did you come home with a whole stack of them?"

A laugh snorted out of Sumatra's nose, but she tried to cover it up with a few coughs.

Meanwhile, Kona changed the subject.

"Brisa?" the violet filly asked right back. "Did *you* figure out what *you're* going to be when you grow up?"

Brisa grinned.

"I'm joining the circus!" she announced.

"The circus!?" Sumatra burst out. "Is that why you're all . . . gluey?"

"I might have had a little accident in the center ring," Brisa said, looking just as shifty-eyed as Kona had a moment earlier. "But that won't stop me! Someday, I'm going to be just as grand a show horse as the great TrixieBelle LaRue, whom I'm *sure* you've heard of. I won't give up, no matter *what* it takes!"

"Oh, really?" Sumatra asked. She had to bite her tongue to keep from laughing this time.

"Oh, yes!" Brisa said earnestly. "My days of lounging on clouds are over! I'm ready to get to work!"

"Well . . . me, too!" Kona said a bit competitively. "Tomorrow, I'm going to pass out *all* my leftover tickets!"

"Then you'd better get ready to give one to me!" Sirocco declared. "For *speeding*. I'm going to be a racehorse!"

Sumatra noticed that Sirocco had very purposefully stopped licking at his wounds and started clopping proudly around the living room.

"So, *that's* how you got so muddy?" Sumatra asked him earnestly. "Winning a horse race? Wow!"

"Winning . . . ?" Sirocco's voice trailed off nervously. Now, *his* eyes were the ones going shifty. "Um, well . . . I didn't have, uh, *time* to make it to the winner's circle. After all, I had to get home to help you all with dinner." And quickly changing the subject, he asked Sumatra about her day.

"My job?" Sumatra asked a bit nervously. "Well, I started off as a cow horse. But then I thought, why settle for just one career?"

"Um, *what* are you talking about?" Brisa asked, blinking in confusion.

"Well, how can I decide on just *one* job when there are so *many* cool ones to dream about?" Sumatra said breezily.

"B-b-but," Kona stammered, "today was our Career Day. *You* sent us out to find our callings!"

"And we all found great ones!" Sumatra replied happily. "Maybe tomorrow or the next day, or the day after that, we'll find more. After all, we've got time. We're young! We're magic! We're Wind Dancers! We can do—and be—*anything*!"

"I guess," Sirocco said. But he was still frowning. "Though it seems like *anything* we do is going to be hard work."

Sirocco hesitated an instant before blurting, "Racehorses have to train a *lot*."

"So do circus horses!" Brisa admitted.

"And police horses have to be so *serious* all the time," Kona couldn't help telling them.

"And it wasn't so easy herding cows today, I have to say," Sumatra admitted.

But then she added: "I have an idea. Play! *That's* our job. For you," she said, pointing her nose at Sirocco, "it's zipping around like a speed demon."

Sumatra nuzzled Brisa next.

"For Brisa, it's getting glammed up and doing acrobatics in air," she said.

Then she gave Kona a giggly nod.

"And Kona's play is bossing around all her friends," she teased. "Maybe someday, all those things will turn *into* jobs, but for now, they—"

"—should just be a whole lot of fun!" Brisa whinnied.

"Right!" Sumatra said. "I mean, we can't just *work* every day!"

"Not even on dinner?" Sirocco asked. "I'm *so* hungry. I didn't even get to eat a hot pretzel at lunch."

"Sirocco's right," Kona said. "We should get *working* on dinner."

And that's just what they did!

Dream Catchers

That night, the Wind Dancers flew to Leanna's yellow farmhouse. Their smiles were big and carefree.

When they arrived, they found Leanna on the porch swing with her little sister, Sara.

"I'm definitely going to be a pastry chef when I grow up," Leanna was saying to her sister. "I mean, mom's already taught me how to make her famous carrot cake."

"But after school, you said you were going to be an astrophysicist," Sara said, planting her toes on the porch rail to give their swing a push.

"I *know*," Leanna said with a giggle. "But the thing is, I don't even know what an astrophysicist is! I *do* know what architects, surgeons, and writers are, though. And I wouldn't mind giving those careers a try—oh! Wait a minute! I forgot!"

"What?" Sara asked.

"Horses!" Leanna declared.

The Wind Dancers' ears pricked up and they smiled at each other. Leanna was talking about them!

"I forgot how much I love horses," Leanna said. "Well, that settles it. I'm going to be a large-animal veterinarian like Dr. Withers."

Sumatra grinned at her friends.

"That's my cue!" she whispered. Using her teeth to nip up the present she'd been holding between her forelegs, she flew to the open window of Leanna's bedroom and went inside. Then she carefully laid something on the little girl's pillow.

It was a tiny journal! The pages were made

of Kona's birch bark and they were bound together with magic ribbons—the exact same pale green ones as in Sumatra's magic halo.

Scratched onto the notebook's cover were two words: *Dream Catcher*.

Inside were written these words: "Here's a place to write down all your hopes and dreams for your future career. No matter *how* many jobs you think up!"

With that, Sumatra was ready to go to dreamland herself!

She rejoined her friends, and the four of them flitted into the darkening evening.

Laughing and whinnying, they loop-de-looped through the air. They were as carefree as dandelion seeds bouncing on the breeze—and *just* as full of possibilities!

Here's a sneak preview of *Wind Dancers* Book 8:

Hungry as a Horse

CHAPTER 1
If You Give a Horse a Muffin . . .

It was morning in the Wind Dancers' apple tree house, and that meant Sirocco was on clean-up duty from an apple muffin breakfast.

First, he took the breakfast dishes to the water trough and scrubbed them splashily. (Kona sighed good-naturedly and dried the floor with a dandelion fluff mop. Sirocco didn't notice.)

Then, Sirocco used his teeth to stack the breakfast plates on a shelf. (He also failed to spot Brisa straightening them into a neater, prettier stack.)

Finally, the golden colt blew all the crumbs off the table with a few gusts of hot breath. (And once again, he had no idea when Sumatra swept the crumbs from the floor with her pale green tail.)

With his chores finished, Sirocco blew his yellow-gold forelock out of his eyes, and said, "*Whew!* What's on the menu for our mid-morning snack?"

Kona gaped.

Brisa gasped.

But Sumatra spoke up!

"Mid-morning snack?" she asked. "You still have apple muffin crumbs around your mouth!"

"I *know*, but look at this kitchen!" Sirocco said. "It's sparkling! And all because of *my* hard work."

"Oh, *really*? *Your* hard work?" Sumatra asked dryly, while Brisa tittered and Kona rolled her eyes.

"Well, yeah!" the clueless colt said innocently. "And hard work always makes me *extra* hungry!"

Then he turned to Kona.

"You know," he said generously, "I don't need something different for my snack. I'll just take a couple more of those yummy muffins you made for breakfast. We'll call it seconds."

"More like *fourths*!" Kona said. "Besides, there aren't any muffins *left* from breakfast. Not after you ate three whole ones already. You eat food as fast as I can make it!"

"*Hmm,*" Sirocco said, pondering this problem. Then, his brown eyes lit up!

"I have a solution!" he said. "Sumatra and Brisa should help you more often with the cooking. Then you could make more food!"

The three fillies gaped at each other.

"I have a *better* solution," the violet-black Wind Dancer said to Sirocco through gritted teeth. "How about *you* start doing some cooking yourself?"

"*Me*?!" Sirocco squawked.

"Yes, you!" Brisa chimed.

"*Please,*" Sirocco scoffed. "Isn't it enough that I help with the cleaning up around here? I'm not going to *cook*, too. That's filly's work! I'm a *colt*!"